MY LITTLE EYE

BY CURTIS VOISIN AND SERENA TAM

 FriesenPress

Suite 300 - 990 Fort St
Victoria, BC, V8V 3K2
Canada

www.friesenpress.com

ISBN
978-1-5255-9374-1 (Hardcover)
978-1-5255-9373-4 (Paperback)
978-1-5255-9375-8 (eBook)

Juvenile Fiction, Social Themes

Distributed to the trade by The Ingram Book Company

Dedicated to Our Son Theodore Voisin

What Others May See as Weakness is Your Superpower

With my little eye,
I like to play pretend

Like hide and seek
and games with friends

My favourite game of all isn't jumping,
skipping or playing ball,

It's finding things
that mean so much but
can be so small

It's finding things that not everyone sees

Like helping
hands carrying
groceries

I think you know it, let's say it out loud
But first close one eye and make me proud!

I spy with my little eye, someone who is...

Helping Mom and Dad
put dishes away,

A kind friend who always shares
when we play

Making sure to say all
their thank yous and pleases

A classmate who never
hurts you or teases

My little eye may be a little different you see

It's smaller than the other but I'll hope you'll agree...

While it may not be able
to see red, purple or blue

It can see the good inside
of me and you

About Theodore

Theodore is an energetic, goofy and curious little boy. He loves paw patrol, big trucks, roaring like a lion, going fast in his little red car during family walks and making us laugh non-stop. He's just like any other little boy with one exception...

When he was born, we learned that his left eye is affected by an irregularity called **Microphthalmia** which impacts the physical development of his eye which is why his eyes appear to be different in size throughout the book. Often this is also paired with **Coloboma** which means that he is missing pieces of tissues in structures that form that eye. In some cases, Coloboma affects the iris which is recognizable by a keyhole appearance and does not lead to vision loss. In Theodore's case, the retina has been impacted which means that it's very likely that he has little to no vision in this eye and that cannot be corrected with glasses or contact lenses. We're extremely grateful that he has one eye with full vision as not all people have his ability.

We wrote this book because we know that as parents, we have the opportunity to change the narrative around how children view themselves and their peers that are differently-abled. We know that Theodore and other children like him will encounter comments that cause him to feel different and left out. The goal of "My Little Eye" is to reframe how differently-abled children view what makes them unique. Our wish is that Theodore and children like him will be reminded of their own hidden superpowers if hurtful comments are made or if they are in need of an extra confidence boost.

Theodore is our superhero and we're excited that you chose this book out of thousands of others to share with your child. We hope that this book starts meaningful conversations that lead to learning, building empathy and most of all; we hope that you find joy in the pleasure of spending time nurturing young minds through reading. Thanks for taking the time to learn and share in Theodore's journey.

Thank You for Your Contribution

5% of your proceeds are going to Sick Kids Foundation
www.sickkidsfoundation.com

5% is supporting the Vision Institute of Canada
www.visioninstitutecanada.com

We'd love to hear from you so please feel free to drop us a line
through our website at **www.mylittleeye.ca**.
If you like **My Little Eye**, please consider sharing this link
with friends. We appreciate your support.

CPSIA information can be obtained
at www.ICGtesting.com
Printed in the USA
BVHW020025120521
607056BV00016B/2120